When They Came Back

A Horror Story

Text by Christopher Conlon
Photographs by Roberta Lannes-Sealey

When They Come Back: A Horror Story
Text by Christopher Conlon
Photographs by Roberta Lannes-Sealey
Text copyright © 2014 Christopher Conlon
Photographs copyright © 2014 Roberta Lannes-Sealey
Edited by Michael J. Hayde

Published in the USA by:
BearManor Media
P O Box 71426
Albany, Georgia 31708
www.bearmanormedia.com

ISBN: 978-1-59393-394-4
Printed in the United States of America
Book design by Robbie Adkins

1.

When they came back
it was the night of black rain
after the day of black rain
when farmers reached their palms
to what fell from the luminous
green clouds turbulent
above them to find their flesh
covered with dark streaks,
like oil but not really:
more solid, beads of black mercury.
No one had ever seen rain like that
in Hardgrove, Nebraska, Jackson
County, in the Year of Our Lord 1899,
or any other year, or any other
place. The mud it made
seemed to glisten and glow.
Cows hid from it in barns, and horses.
Children ran out to play, only to turn again
to their houses, complain to their mothers
that it burned. It rained all day like that
and through the night. It was still raining
when they came back.

2.

Gideon Boone opened his door at midnight
to a knock. Nobody ever knocked.
He lived miles from anyone. There
in the lamplight was his wife Obedience—
Biddie—her pale blue dress torn
and smeared with filth. It was the dress
they were to bury her in on Sunday. Her face
was sunken, starved, her cheeks
worm-white and hollow; her eyes dim
black pebbles. (They had been blue, too.)
Her golden hair was askew, like that
of a madwoman, spraying out
in all directions, clumped with mud.
She reeled, nearly fell. Her mouth
moved, gaping, as if trying to capture
air, or to speak. Her palms, sheened
with black rain, opened as if beseeching
her husband of thirty years to tell her
what she was doing there. Boone drew back
into the kitchen, stumbled against the table
he'd built for her long ago, fell
into a chair, wordless, worldless.

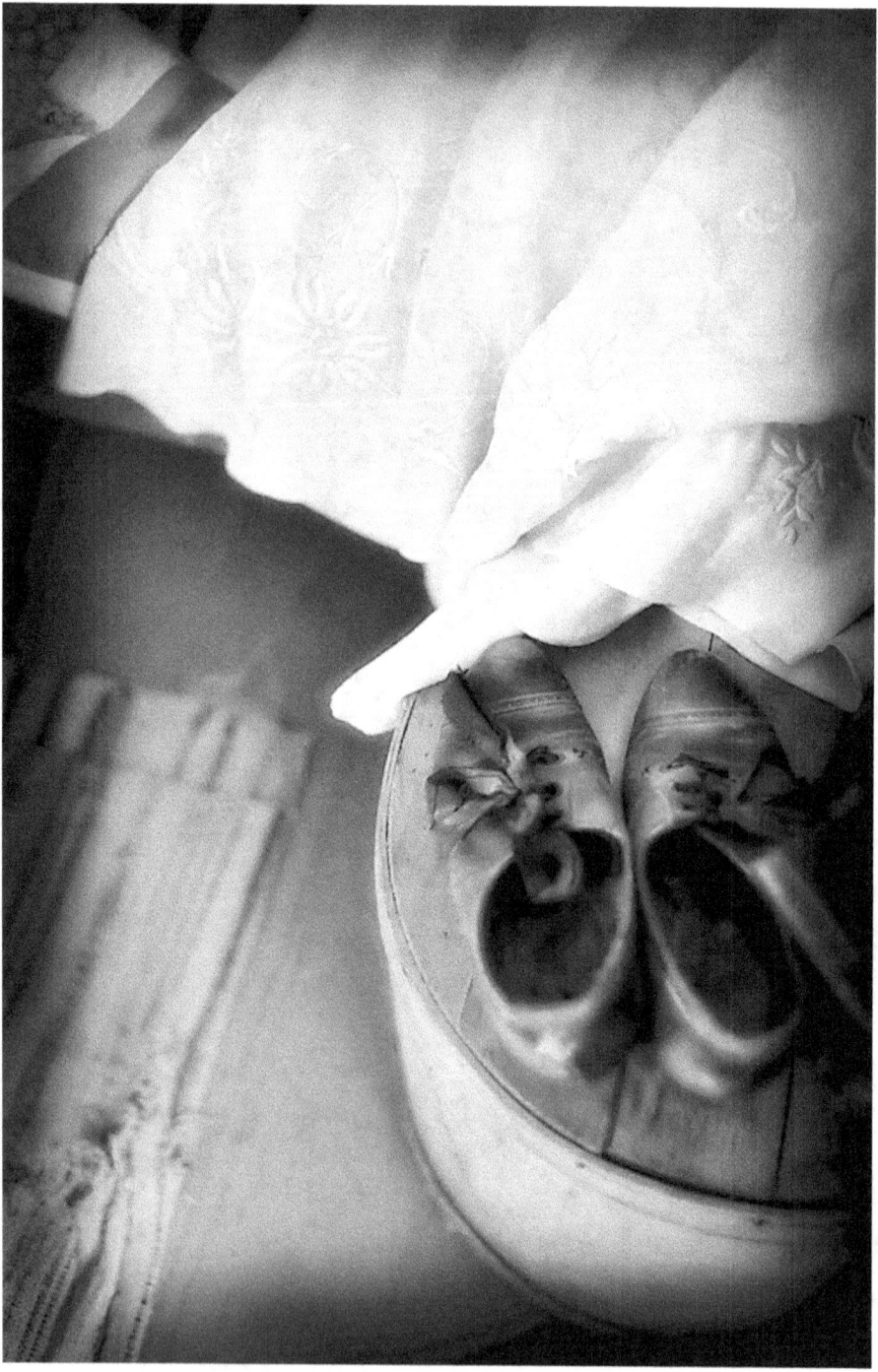

3.

Olivia Wheeler stood at the foot of her sister's
bed in the attic room they'd shared. Waking
to darkness, Winifred, aged eight, saw her
blackglowing in the night and sat up wide-eyed.
"Livy?" Lightning flashed, odd,
green-tinged, and Winnie saw for an instant
Livy's sick countenance—dark pockets
under her eyes, blue and black shadows
smothering her neck, shoulders, face.
She wore her white nightgown, streaked black
now like bruised tears. "Livy!"
Winnie leapt from bed, hugging the silent
girl. She kissed the cold cheeks,
grasped the cold hands in her own.
She'd not known such happiness
ever in her life, even if Livy's eyes
seemed dark, distant. Still, it was *her.*
"Livy, Livy, Livy!" Then quickly,
holding her close, she pressed her finger
to her sister's dry lips. "Shh. Shh.
Father mustn't know you've come back.
He'll do it again, Livy. He'll do it again."

4.

The stranger woke at the side of the train tracks,
mind cluttered, bewildered. He had an image
of walking down this dirt path under roiling clouds,
past the spiderwort and meadow rose, then
an image of falling—dropping
to the soft junegrass, his bag of belongings
spilling out beside him, something in his chest
shattered. Then nothing. Then this: darkness,
black rain, uneasy confusion. He knew
his things in the bag, knew his shirts and socks
and tobacco, but had words for none of them,
nor for *road* or *walk* or *rain* or even *I*.
He stood, bones and muscles slow, moved fumblingly
to gather his gear, stepped to the road
and followed it, a dim impression
flickering within him of something ahead, a town,
though he had no word for *town*, no word
for anything. Lightning flashed strangely, unlike
anything he thought he'd seen. Rain stretched
blackly from the brim of his hat to his cheeks.
He lurched forward, peering into the dark
for something. A face, a word. Himself. *I*.

5.

Restless with the heavy splattering of rain
on his roof, Father Synge rose, lit his old tin lantern,
decided to step into his office—the house
was connected to the rear of the church—and work
on the eulogy for poor Mrs. Boone, gone much
too early, Lord's will be done. Toting the lantern
in one hand he made his way down the dark
corridor and into the main building, black
but for his small light, the downpour thunderous
around him. Her pine coffin was there,
ready for burial Sunday. But the shadows around it
were wrong. Stepping close he saw that it was
open, and empty. Impossible! Dr. Thorne
had finished with her yesterday, had dropped
the lid softly over her and departed. He rubbed
his sleep-stubbled cheek. (Why, why
was the cloudburst so infernally loud?)
He noticed strands of hair then, long gold,
caught in the coffin lid's hinge. He stepped
through the hall and into the church
itself. The pulpit was dim, and the pews.
The front door gaped open in the rain.

6.

Biddie fell heavily when she tried to sit
next to her husband and he leapt up,
helped her in the semi-dark to the chair.
Her skin was cold, but she'd walked long miles
in the tempest, obviously slipped repeatedly
in mud. She must be terribly sick.
"Biddie?" he said under the sound of rain.
"Biddie, how have you come here? I saw...
I thought I saw...the minister, Biddie, and the
doctor, they said...you'd been so very ill..."
Kneeling before her, he touched her wet hand,
stroked her forearm. The texture was
strange, like paper that's been wet and then dried
again. Uneven, mottled like that. He looked up
into her eyes and saw no light at all, only darkness.
"Biddie, do you know me? Gideon Boone,
your husband?" Her head turned. "Biddie, we must
get you to a doctor, but it's impossible tonight.
The storm, you see." He gestured to the black-smeared
window. Then, voice husky, eyes stinging
and wet, he said, "My Lord, Biddie, I love you so."
He took her wrist and held it. She had no pulse.

7.

Winnie lit a candle. In the fluttering light she
stepped close to her little sister and whispered.
"Livy? You must put on something dry. Here,
give me your dress." The girl did not move.
"Livy? Come." She reached to the sodden, filthy
material, pulled it gently over her sister's
head. Livy did not resist. She stood there naked
in the candle's quivering glow while Winnie picked
a nightgown for her from the bureau, thick socks, underpants.
She held them out for her sister who did not respond, looked
dully at her, no emotion discernable except, perhaps,
puzzlement. To Winnie her eyes seemed dim
and wrong. She tried to press the clothing into her hands
but the girl stumbled, nearly fell. "Sit down, sit."
Livy dropped to the edge of the bed. Winnie
put the things over her sister's feet and privates
and adjusted the gown on her shoulders.
Finally it was all straight. "Livy, Livy," she whispered,
tears choking her, pulling her sister down onto the pillow
with her, as she would after the poor thing had suffered
another of Father's terrible thrashings, and they would breathe
together in the dark. But Livy was not breathing now.

8.

For a while, sitting under the awning of the shuttered saloon, bottle in hand, Cyrus Drain wasn't sure it was real: through the night's black fury a man seemed to be approaching town, far off down the main street, now clogged mud. His vision was foggy, the storm strong, but there he was, yes, a *man*, tall, rail-thin, brown coat and hat, denim pants, some sort of rucksack over his shoulder, and no protection at all from the squall. The man swayed this way and that, fell to one knee, stood, lurched forward. Was he drunk? Why didn't he take shelter? Cyrus Drain watched as the man came nearer, slipped, fell again, this time seemingly trapped in the gleaming slime, too weak or intoxicated to move. Why, he might die there!

Cyrus moved quickly, surprisingly so for the town lush. He stepped toward him, stinging rain pelting his skin, calling, "Mister? Sir?" No response, but the man did jerk a little, spasmodically. The rucksack was fallen at his side. Cyrus leaned down, peered into it, could see nothing in this damnable tempest. So he tossed the whole bag over his shoulder and rifled the man's coat, found a silver dollar, a jack knife, pocketed them. "Oughtn't to drink so much, stranger," he advised, voice all but lost in the rain. "Terrible things can happen." Chuckling, he disappeared into the dark.

9.

The next morning was clear and bright
in Hardgrove, Nebraska, population 260,
elevation 2543. Mr. Sandstone opened
his Emporium & General Goods Store
as usual, Mr. Bailey his Farm & Feed Store,
Mr. Kreiger his blacksmith's shop. Miss String
unlocked the front door and stepped in
for another day at the only public library
within a hundred miles. It was cold, hardly
above freezing, but mild for this time
of year. In the sunlight most traces
of the night's storm had vanished. The roads
were still muddy, but no one noticed any
glimmer or glow. Red-winged blackbirds fluttered
on telegraph lines. A pair of brown hawks
lazily circled the blue sky. A few early patrons
of Mr. Henry's Tavern slouched in, ordered their
morning constitutionals, commented on the fierce
weather of the night before: "Did it look *off* to you?
Black, sorta?" It did, but then it was a dark night.
Drinks in hand, they moved on to more pressing
topics. McKinley. Taxation. The price of corn.

10.

Father Synge considered walking to the sheriff's office
that morning, but instead hitched up his wagon
with Bessie and Blue and began the long ride
to Gideon Boone's house. He was heartsick
and tried to rehearse in his mind just how he
would tell him: *Mr. Boone, I am so dreadfully sorry*
to have to say this, but it appears that grave robbers
entered the church last night and removed poor dear...
It was a ghastly thing to have to speak. Body snatchers,
here? In Hardgrove? Who ever heard of such a thing?
Surely it was the Devil's work. Father Synge
shut his eyes briefly, felt the icy morning air on his face. He
would drive the distraught man to the sheriff, of course.
But when he arrived at the house and knocked, Boone
opened the door only a crack, an odd, lopsided smile
on his face. The minister cleared his throat, spoke.
"Thank you, sir," Boone said, well before he'd
finished. "I shall attend to the matter." And the man
shut the door in his face. As Father Synge turned
to depart, he noticed indistinct footprints, as from
a woman's small shoes, leading to Boone's front door.
There were no footprints leading away.

11.

In the light of day Winnie knew how sick
her sister was. Her skin was pale yellow, her eyes
shadowed, her dirt-crusted hair came out
in clumps when Winnie tried to brush it. And she
did nothing but sit silently in a chair staring
at the wall. Livy must have a doctor. But how
could she get to town to bring him
without Father knowing, since he didn't
even allow Winnie to go to school anymore?
She whispered, "Stay here, stay quiet," though
there was no need. Livy made no sound, anyway.
Winnie dressed, stepped downstairs and out
to the chickens. She took up a bucket
and began collecting the eggs. Livy would need
food, she knew, as well as a doctor. There were
so many problems. She wished they could just
live there together without Father at all,
just the two of them. Winnie
would do all the work if Livy was too sick....
As she picked up another warm egg she heard
a sound. Was it from upstairs? Where was Father?
She dropped the bucket. She ran toward the house.

12.

////nowhere at all in///darkness in///
breathlessness///mumbled sounds///distant
voice//no words for ////anything only
sensation///*pain*///pulled his face
from black//////muck something hit
/////his head /////dirt down his neck but
no words only///hurt numb//itching/////
look///around him circling braying
boys///one no front teeth one
freckles////one scars on fat
cheeks////laughing throwing big hard
clods////shouting *He's drunk*
he's drunk///*his mother kissed a skunk*/////
all just sound light////motion no///meaning
just//danger///stood slowly children//////
scattering like////hyenas////world tilted
slammed into////shoulder laughing//sound
tried///to pick up//////bag//////////but
nothing try/////////////comprehend////
what's///near him//////what//
nothing/////cold///nothing//////pain
/////////nothing///////////nothing///////

13.

Something was odd, thought Morris Levitt,
about today. He watched boys abusing a drunken
stranger in the street, shooed them off. Observed
that aged reprobate Cyrus Drain on a back street
with a big bag in his hand, looking even more
furtive than he generally did. Saw the Reverend
riding out of town toward nothing at all except
maybe old Boone's place. No one else was out there.
And the rain, last night's rain. He searched the
streets and gutters, saw little trace of what had fallen
in the dark, perhaps just the hint of some dim obsidian
glow. As the editor of the *Jackson County Chronicle*
he needed to learn what he could. He asked around
at Mr. Sandstone's store, stepped into Miss String's
library for a moment, but no one had anything to say.
Finally he strode to the telegraph office and sent
a message to Davis, the reporter at Blue Mesa,
next town over as the crow flies, the wind blows.
ANY BLACK RAIN THERE STOP. An answer,
brought to him two hours later by a boy:
NO RAIN ALL WELL STOP. Morris sifted
black dirt through his fingers, and wondered.

14.

When Winnie reached the front steps the door
banged open and Father was there, eyes wide,
mouth gaping. He smelled like whiskey, as he
usually did. He looked at his older daughter
but it was as if he didn't see her, as if
she weren't there at all. "Can't," he said under
his breath. "Can't be. No, it can't be."
He stumbled off the porch steps and turned
to the side of the house, made his way
toward the hill behind, tearing his way through
the long prairie grass. Winnie knew where
he was going. She stepped into the house,
ran upstairs. "Livy, what happened, what
happened?" But she was still in her chair,
unchanged. Her head turned when her sister
came in, that's all. Winnie moved to the window
and looked at Father mounting the hill. He
fell once, twice, finally made it to what she saw
was now an open hole in the ground, a shallow
depression of dirt where anyone could see
that something had once been hastily buried.
A dog, maybe. A calf. A baby pig. A girl.

15.

After the preacher departed Gideon Boone
turned to his wife again. The morning sun
made dust motes glow gold in the still room.
She was sitting where he'd left her,
in the tub he'd placed in the middle
of the floor. The water steamed. He
crouched before her again, took the old cloth
and dunked it in the water, wrung it out,
gently soaked her forehead with it, her
eyelids, her cheeks and nose, her lips,
her ears. With her eyes closed she seemed
almost as she'd been, as he remembered her
for the past thirty years. He could believe
she would be all right, she was merely
ill, very ill, with her husband's care
she would improve. He bathed her shoulders
and back, her arms, her breasts. He would not
farm today. He would not do anything today.
He could not stop crying. He knew it was
impossible to take her to Dr. Thorne in town,
that the old quack would say, "She needs
no medical attention. This woman is dead."

16.

Sheriff Ryder made his way outside
after little Bobby Wright came into the office
saying a dead man was lying in the street.
The stranger was in the street all right, but
he was moving, flailing about. Drunk
was what he was. "Hey, stranger," the sheriff
called, "how 'bout you getttin' up
out of the road? Make it easy so I can
arrest you." But the man didn't respond,
flopped this way and that. Ryder leaned down
and pulled at his arm, dragged him up
out of the muck. "C'mon," he said. "What's
your name?" The stranger staggered. Ryder
caught his arm again. "Well, you can sleep it off
in the jail. This is a respectable town,
mister." The sheriff supported the stranger
as he took him in, dropped him onto a bench
in the cell and shut the door. Later
he found himself wondering at the sweet,
putrid odor in his office that put him off
his coffee. Maybe a rat died
in a drawer somewhere. He'd have to check.

17.

Winnie watched as her father
backed away from the dirt,
looked toward the house, backed
away farther, held his hand
to his mouth, shook his head.
Then he moved, stalking quickly
away, cresting the hill
and vanishing. She knew
that he was going to Mr. Henry's
Tavern, a little more than a mile
away. She knew he would drink there,
think, drink some more. She knew
that when he returned he would be
in a furious mood, stumbling, eyes
red, voice loud and slurred. She knew
he would start beating Livy then.
She knew she had to get Livy away because
he would grab her by the neck, shake
and choke her, pummel her with his fists,
scream that she had *killed his wife,*
murdered her mother, even though
living was Livy's only sin.

18.

Boone asked her to shut her eyes
as he carried her up the stairs
to their bedroom. It was her eyes, her
lightless eyes that were the hardest
to bear. Her strange skin, her odor, her
heartbeat—symptoms of some peculiar,
profound malady. But if her eyes remained
closed she was with him again, as they'd been
for so many years. He placed her gently
on the bed. Sunshine poured through the
window, illuminated her in gold. He
removed his clothing, lay beside her.
She turned her head to him, eyes shut,
accepted his caresses passively, not
as she had before. He touched
her, kissed her, told her how
he loved her. When he
mounted her at last, her arms
moved for the first time, and her legs,
weakly rising, feebly embracing
him, obeying instincts of thirty years,
memories deeper than brain or bone.

19.

Miss String locked the library door
behind her at twelve o'clock, as
she always did, made her way across
the cold street to Sheriff Ryder's office
with her lunch basket to share. They
enjoyed sandwiches and fruit together
twice weekly, had for the past year.
She'd fixed chicken this time, on hard
brown bread, and had bought two small
red apples, unlikely to be sweet,
but the best that could be found
this time of year in Hardgrove. She knocked
demurely, though she knew she
was expected, opened the door, and was met
with a terrible stench. "Sheriff Ryder,"
she said, "what on earth is that odor?"
He said he'd tried but couldn't discover
the source. "We can't eat here," she said firmly,
"please, come to the library." As they walked
Miss String surreptitiously leaned to the sheriff,
sniffed, reassured herself that the smell
was not him. It could be nothing living, anyway.

20.

Winnie found an old burlap sack
and began tossing things into it,
clothes, shoes, books, food,
saying, "Livy, we must go! As
far as we can! Before Father
gets back! Put on your coat, Livy!"
But Livy's coat was gone, as
she'd been, until last night.
Winnie had another, wrapped
her sister in it, gave her a spare
scarf and gloves too. "Come, come!"
She tried to pick up the bag
but discovered it was far too
heavy to carry. She wept
in frustration, pulled out items,
piled them on the floor, tried
to tote the bag again, again failed,
abandoned more possessions.
By the time she had something
she could carry she was left with nearly
nothing. She pulled Livy along, escaped
to the roofless shelter of cold day.

21.

Boone lay for a long time
next to his wife, shoulder to
shoulder, hand in hand.
He listened for her breathing
as he'd heard it for
thirty years, but heard nothing.
And yet she'd responded,
she loved him somewhere
in her broken mind and body.
She'd come through the rain
last night, after all, to him,
to their life together again. But
her silence frightened
him. Her motionlessness
worried him. Her smell. He
wondered how long they could
live like this, how long it'd be
until people came, the
preacher, the sheriff,
asking questions. He stroked
his wife's hand, knew joy,
pleasure, anxiety, terror.

22.

After an excellent lunch with Miss String—
so pretty, so intelligent, though he knew
he had no chance with her (he was uneducated,
gruff, lacked her gentle refinement, her way
with words)—the sheriff returned to his office
in an expansive mood which was instantly
snuffed when he opened the door
and remembered the stench. It was too cold
to open the windows, but as he stepped
into the room he suspected immediately
what had seemed unthinkable: it was
his prisoner, the drunken loafer. He
walked up to the man, studied him
as he sat there unmoving on the bench.
"You feelin' good enough to go, mister?"
he asked. Anything, he thought,
to rid the office of the stink! He unlocked
the door and the man stood. "If you can walk
a straight line, you're free." Ryder felt a chill,
a goose on his grave, as the stranger passed him
by, and his mind flooded with images of death:
his, the stranger's, Miss String's, the world's.

23.

Lucas Wheeler sat in Mr. Henry's Tavern
pondering the impossible. He'd buried the bitch
himself, disposed of all her belongings.
That couldn't have been her sitting there
in Winnie's bedroom. It was a ghost,
an hallucination. He kicked back his shot
and called for another, his fifth
or sixth, he'd lost count. The longer he sat
the more he became convinced that he'd seen
nothing at all in the bedroom. But what
of the hole in the ground where she
should have been—ruptured, empty? All
illusion. Madness. Everything was all right.
It had to be. Winnie would have screamed
in terror to see her sister returned like that.
She would have run to Father for protection,
sweet girl. This realization made him so happy
that when Cyrus Drain sidled up to him and said
greasily, "Mr. Wheeler, you appear well-heeled
this afternoon, might you...?" he immediately
called to the bartender, "Sir, a drink
for this fine man! Your very best whiskey!"

24.

In the parsonage at the rear of the church,
Father Synge gently deflected the questions
of the newspaperman, Mr. Levitt. The reporter
hoped to learn why the Reverend had ridden out
in the direction of Gideon Boone's place
that morning. "That's confidential, Mr. Levitt.
I would never discuss matters involving my
parishioners." Morris tried a few minutes longer,
asked also about the strange rain of the night before:
"Did it seem odd to you, Father?" But Synge
merely smiled, shrugged. They stepped out
the side door, a pleasant route back to the
the main street, past the church cemetery.
There were sounds—faint thumpings,
muffled and indistinct, coming from around
the tombstones and crosses. Synge and Levitt
looked at each other. "Father, does that sound
like knocking to you? From under the earth?"
The Reverend swallowed, his mouth dry.
He'd heard the sounds since late last night.
"Young man, that's madness," he said firmly,
leading him quickly away from the graveyard.

25.

They didn't get far. Livy simply couldn't
keep up with her sister, stumbling, lurching
this way and that. The girl could see—she
avoided pits in the path—but acted as if
she were sightless, arms outstretched
before her. At last Winnie pulled them
into the corn, dead brown shafts at this time
of year, half of them leaning over, broken.
They huddled together. Winnie brought
bread from the bag she carried, offered
some to Livy, who ignored it. Winnie ate,
trying not to cry. It was cold
and the wind was beginning to pick up,
sighing through the dry stalks. "Let's
play a game, Livy," she said. "I Spy?
Hop, Step, and Jump?" But she knew Livy
couldn't play those games. Despair sank
into her bones. At last she held up her hands.
"Please play with me, Livy. Come. Pat a cake,
pat a cake, baker's man." It took her sister
a very long time to raise her hands. But
finally, slowly, silently, she did.

26.

Morris Levitt stepped into Mr. Henry's Tavern
and found two unlikely conversationalists,
Lucas Wheeler and Cyrus Drain, discoursing
on the world today. It was Drain, however,
doing most of the talking. "How different it all is
now," he said, kicking back his shot glass. "What
is the world now? It's gone mad. Automobiles,
telephones, moving pictures, gramophones. Too
modern for me, this coming century. Not like
when I was a young buck. It's all...*decadent,* if I may
use such a word. Don't you agree, Mr. Wheeler?"
Wheeler only grunted. Cyrus Drain looked
toward Morris. "Mr. Newspaper Editor," he said,
lurching off the stool toward him, "don't you agree
that this country has become decadent? That we
are now in the end times? That judgment,
fiery, final judgment will soon be upon us?"
Morris looked at the flabby old drunk,
thought of the church cemetery again.
"Yes, Mr. Drain," he said quietly, sincerely,
"I believe that we are most certainly in the
end times, and judgment is sure to follow."

27.

She got out of bed after a while, moved clumsily
to the closet where her clothes had been. "No, Biddie,"
her husband said, following her, "they're not there
now, I had them taken away. I am sorry, my dear. But
a few things are still in this old trunk, favorites
I hadn't the heart to..." He stopped, looked at her,
opened it. He pulled out a white blouse, blue
skirt, helped her with them. She seemed to want
to go downstairs. He supported her, saying, "Careful,
slowly, slowly," and when she arrived she stepped
into the kitchen, opened cupboards, touched spoons
and bowls. Boone watched her, a terrible pain
welling in his throat. "Biddie, there's no need to make us
a meal, you're far too ill." But she kept moving about
restlessly. He knew what she wanted. After lovemaking,
their special daytime lovemaking as they'd done
when they were young, she always made him
griddle cakes— flour, milk, egg, a hot pan sizzling
with butter. For a moment, watching her, he could
almost believe it, believe that the cakes were coming.
Then he stood and said "No, Biddie," guiding her
gently to a chair. "Today I will make the cakes."

28.

From the front window of the library Miss String
observed the stranger from the jail cell shamble slowly
out of the sheriff's office. He moved like no man
she'd ever seen, as if he were drunk but not
exactly. She watched him move up the street
out of sight and, since there were no
patrons at the moment, she slipped on her coat
again, put up her hand-drawn *Librarian
Will Return in 10 Minutes* sign and stepped out,
locked the door, crossed the street to where
she knew Sheriff Ryder would be. The odor had
improved in the room, but what she mostly
noticed was Mr. Ryder leaning against a post,
a strange expression in his eyes. "Frederick?"
she said, saying the name she used only
when they were alone. His eyes came to her
as from a dream. "Miss String," he said, clearing
his throat, "this is hardly the place, but would
you—Leonora, would you do me the honor
of committing to marriage with me?" She smiled,
nerves jumping under her skin. "Why, of course,
Frederick. You might have asked before, you know."

29.

Tired and drunk, Cyrus Drain went back
to the room he rented above Mr. Sandstone's store,
collapsed onto the sagging old bed. He
would get up later, cadge more liquor
at Mr. Henry's until he got himself thrown
out, as happened most nights. He noticed
the bag then, the stranger's rucksack, tossed in
the corner. He'd taken out what had any value—
clothes, mostly—but hadn't bothered to look
at the papers at the bottom. Now, before sleep,
he did. Letters, of no interest. "Dear Father,"
read the one on top, dated days ago, "I
cannot express how much I look forward
to meeting you at last. I am so very grateful
that you responded to my inquiry. With Mother
having passed away I am now quite alone
in the world. Thank you for your offer to help
me. I eagerly await seeing you as planned,
in the lobby of the Knickerbocker Hotel,
Tuesday, at 10:30 a.m. Yours Most Sincerely,
Your Daughter, Anna." Drain crumpled the paper
and tossed it onto the floor, was quickly asleep.

30.

Father Synge waited several hours
for Boone to come into town, but finally
decided to go to the sheriff's office himself.
Rehearsing in his mind how he would
explain what had happened was almost as bad
as it had been with Boone. Why on earth would
anyone steal a corpse here? Where would
they take it? What would they do with it?
Such things happened in cities, with their
medical schools and research hospitals, not
in Hardgrove, Nebraska, population 260.
He stepped up to the door and opened
it. There was a faint odor, sweet, indefinable,
but that's not what surprised him. What surprised
him was the sight of Sheriff Ryder and the librarian,
Miss String, holding hands on the bench.
"We wish to be married," said Ryder, without
preamble, to which the Reverend responded,
"Of course, God be praised, congratulations
to you both. But Sheriff, I must speak with you.
Miss String, would you excuse us, please?
This matter is not, alas, for ladies' ears."

31.

Boone fried the griddle cakes, not as well
as Biddie would have done. At first the butter
was too cool, then too hot. Some of the cakes
were scorched. But finally he mastered it,
flipped cakes energetically, set a handsome stack
on the table, discarded the bad ones. He
served up three to Biddie, who sat there
unmoving, three to himself. He'd made
coffee as well, and he poured two cups,
added sugar. "Eat, Biddie, do," he said,
"you must build up your strength." But she
could get no farther than clumsily spearing
a bit of cake, moving it toward the vicinity
of her mouth, dropping it to the plate
again. Boone moved his chair closer
and attempted to help her, holding the fork
himself, trying to feed her, but her mouth
would not open to accept the food or drink.
She seemed to scowl, her expression appeared
to grow perplexed. Her head turned toward
her husband, cocked, inquiring, as if to ask,
What am I to do, and why don't I remember?

32.

Morris Levitt drank in Mr. Henry's Tavern
for a while longer, happy that Cyrus Drain
had gone and Lucas Wheeler had submerged
into silence. He could not get the sound
he'd heard in the church graveyard out of his mind.
It was so fantastical that he began to wonder
if he'd heard it at all, if it was possible that
he'd heard something else. A door banging
in the breeze. Someone hammering
somewhere. The Reverend had denied it,
called it madness, and surely it was. He tried
not to picture waking in a coffin, darkness
beyond darkness, airless, comfortless,
and then the moment of realization, the frantic
banging, the screaming, the clawing
at the lining and wood, the realization that
no one was coming to save you. He closed
his eyes, tried not to hear the thumping
in his mind, tried not to remember who was in
that cemetery. His father. His beloved mother,
of sainted memory. His brother John, dead
of a kick to the ear by a horse, aged eight.

33.

It was late afternoon when Sheriff Ryder,
having left Miss String, *Leonora*, back
at her library with a quick squeeze
to her gloved hands and a smile, trudged
to the church with Father Synge, learned
exactly nothing. An empty coffin. No
evidence of anything except that the church's
front door was open in the night. He
tried to think of who would steal a body,
Mrs. Boone's, anyone's, and why. "You'll
need to file a report," he said. "Though
more properly Mr. Boone should file it.
Stolen property. In the meantime I'll look
around, ask some questions." Father Synge
thanked him and he left. Walking back
up the street, an absurd thought slid into
his mind. Leonora had said, "You know,
Frederick, that prisoner of yours smelled as if
he were dead. Like some awful Poe story." So corpses
were up and moving about the streets of Hardgrove?
He shook his head, annoyed with himself. No.
Edgar Allan Poe was not welcome in his town.

34.

When school let out Miss String's library
received a flurry of patrons, mostly girls. She
studied them as they fluttered about the shelves,
thinking of how much she loved children,
wondering if it would prove too late to have
one of her own. She could hardly contain
her happiness, wanted to jump and shout
in a decidedly unladylike manner, wished
she could gather the girls together and make
the announcement to them, listen to them
shriek and giggle over it. When she'd asked him
what caused his sudden resolution to propose,
he'd said: "I had a vision, Leonora. I seemed
to see in my mind all the days of my life,
the future days, and how lonely they would be
without you. It happened as I released
the prisoner. I don't know why. All I know
is that I want to spend what remains of my life
with you." She smiled, checked out an adventure
story for a girl, smiled again. The dead-smelling
stranger skated over her mind only
a moment, was obliterated in her bright joy.

35.

As the sun began to set, Livy
stood suddenly, turned away from
her sister, began walking in
a different direction. Winnie
called to her, stepped up
to her, took her sleeve. "Livy?
What are you doing? Where are
you going?" But the girl
just kept walking, stumbling
occasionally, through the dead
corn and out into the cold
prairie grass, along the gentle hill
behind the house. After
some minutes Winnie began
to suspect, cried, "Livy, no, *no*,"
but the girl kept on walking,
moving slowly toward the other
hill, the one Winnie had seen
her father on before. They
climbed it clumsily. Soon
it was in view, the open hole
like a violent wound in the earth.

36.

Light failed and the air
grew colder. The stranger
staggered toward the train tracks
outside town, though nobody
saw him. Sheriff Ryder
locked the office and
headed toward his boardinghouse
for supper. Miss String did
the same after she closed
the library, making her way
down darkening streets
in the other direction, to the
women-only establishment
run by old Mrs. Fenster. The
reporter, Morris Levitt,
sat drinking, watched
as Lucas Wheeler lumbered
out of the tavern toward,
he supposed, home.
Father Synge prayed.
Cyrus Drain slept.
The night sky grew strange.

37.

As a glowing darkness dropped
through the air, Boone cleaned
the dishes and read to his wife
for a while, first from the Bible,
then *Pilgrim's Progress*, a
favorite of them both. He lit
a lamp as twilight faded from
the windows. Finally he said,
"Biddie, we must go to bed now,
I'm sure you're very tired, as
sick as you are." They climbed
the stairs slowly, and again
Boone helped her with her things.
As they got into bed he tried to think
of what tomorrow would be,
and the day after. He could imagine
nothing. He slept uneasily, had what
he thought were dreams of her moving
about, clumsily pulling on
her clothes, stepping out
of the bedroom and the house
finally, forever.

38.

Morris Levitt hardly noticed how odd
the sky seemed as he made his way
from the tavern toward the church
graveyard again, though it did register
in his mind that the encroaching dark
seemed different, somehow. He opened
the little creaking gate that led
to the cemetery and went through it.
As he approached the plain tombstones
and elaborate marble angels he
was sure he heard it—hardly, but
heard it—yet he kept moving, having
drunk just enough to be able to do it.
Arriving finally at the Levitt stones,
he looked down at *Joshua*, his father,
John, his young brother, and finally
his mother, *Sarah*. He leaned down
to her at last, spread his arms
over her grave, pressed his ear
to the earth. Dear God, she was knocking
at the inside of her coffin! Frantically,
with his bare hands, he began digging.

39.

It was after supper, when he stepped outside
for a smoke, that Sheriff Ryder saw the lights
in the sky. For a moment he could not conceive
that he was looking at the stars: they appeared
as no stars he was familiar with. The entire sky
was different, indescribable. It was dark
but not black, not any color he had ever
seen. The stars were there, the familiar
constellations—Big Dipper, Orion's Belt—
but they looked different, not the bright white
he knew, but rather some darker illumination.
That was it: The stars were darker than
the sky itself, as in some photographic
negative. He stood, staring up. What
in God's name was happening? He stepped
in for a moment, gathered his gloves and hat,
set forth once more to town. He had no
idea what was wrong, but something was.
He would open the office again, no one would
have to come to the boardinghouse to find him.
He would light lamps. He would let everyone
know that Sheriff Ryder was on the job.

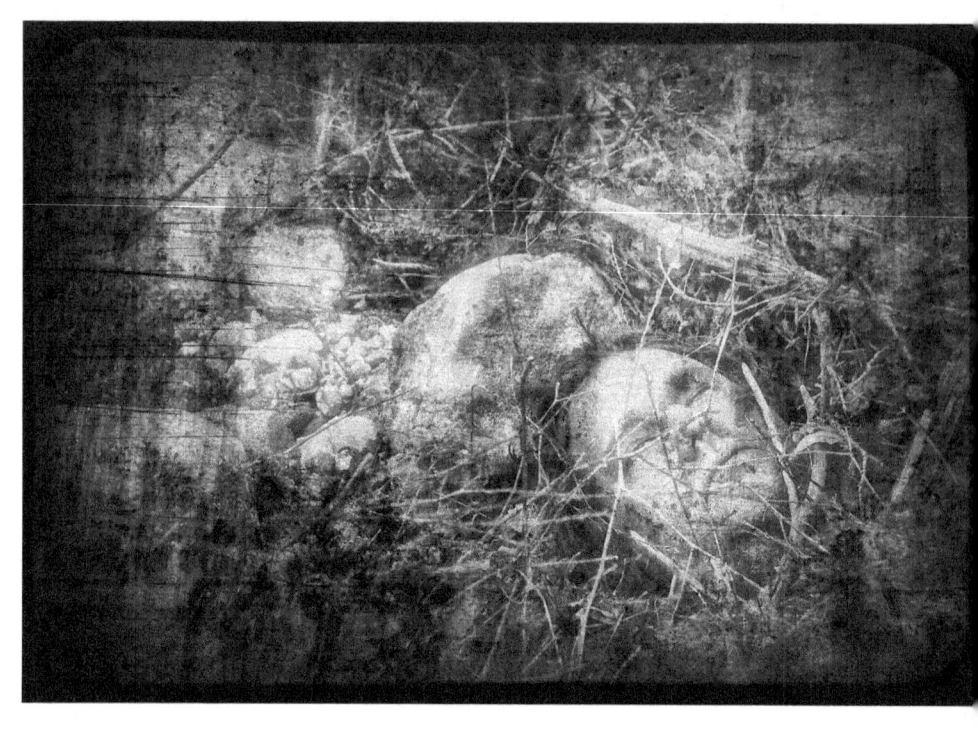

40.

Winnie stood at the open gash
in the earth, noticing the fantastical
sky above her, watching her sister.
Livy stood with her head toward
what had been her grave. She
got on her knees, moved her hands
into the earth, as if she wanted
to return to it. "Livy, Livy,"
Winnie cried, going to her,
taking her by the shoulders,
"no, Livy, I want you with me,
I want us to be together always!
I'll help you through your sickness,
Livy! I'll take care of you! Please,
Livy!" But the girl kept scooping
at the dirt with her hands, too weak
to really accomplish anything, but
it was clear what she meant to do. Winnie
wept into her sister's neck. When
she looked up again her father
was standing before them, blotting out
the mad sky, shotgun cradled in his arms.

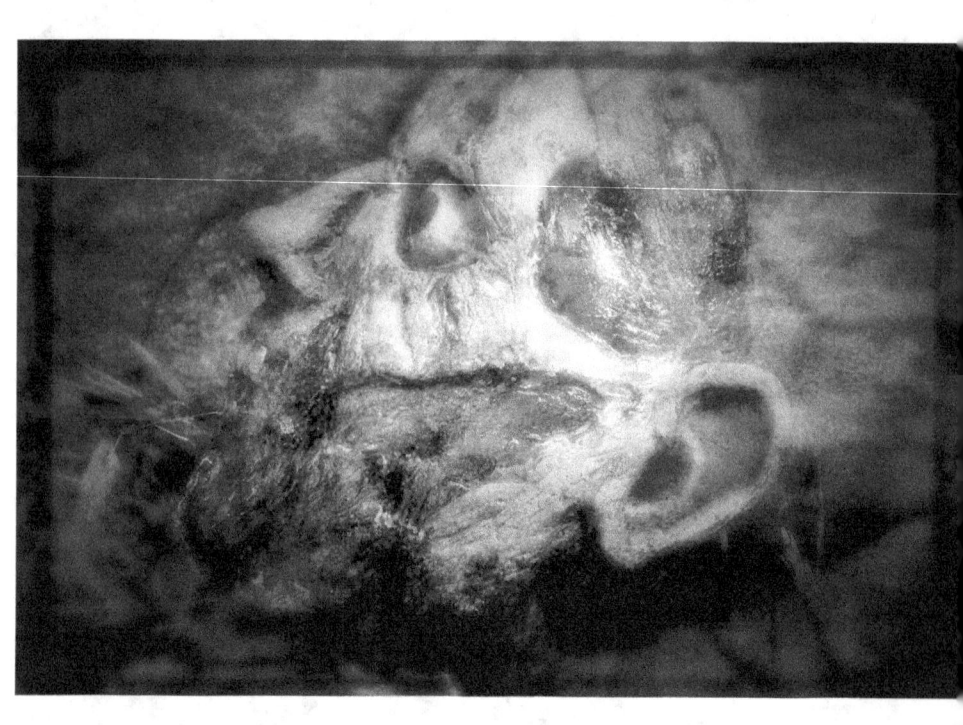

41.

The stranger
shambled
forward, perceiving
dimly
the tracks ahead.
He did not see
the sky, had no
words for
anything he saw
or didn't,
but there were
tiny jolts
in his brain
like electrical
currents of memory.
////girl's face//////
///long road//////
/////black////rain/////

Anna.

////standing after
falling/////falling
//////forever/////

42.

People came out of their houses
that night to stare at the strange
sights above them. They wrapped
themselves in coats and gloves
and looked up. Some discussed
the black rain of the night
before, wondered if there were any
connection. The stars looked
black, at that. No one could name
the color of the sky itself. Cyrus Drain,
having been awakened by talk
outside, opened his window
and looked blearily into
the night. Father Synge knelt
in his church, prayed. Miss String
put herself together well enough
to appear in the street, hear
the whispers, find Frederick,
who said, "Leonora, I don't know."
It grew windy. Someone said they
thought they heard a shot somewhere,
but no one else was listening.

43.

Winnie stood between Livy and the man
with the shotgun. "No," she pleaded,
"you can't." Father muttered, "She killed
your mother. Get out of the way." Livy
backed up, arms outstretched, stumbling,
making the only sound Winnie ever heard
her make: a kind of clicking noise, almost
as if she were strangling, "Khk! Khk!"
"Father," Winnie pleaded, "Livy was *born*,
that's all! It wasn't her fault!" She leapt
at the gun, pointed now at her sister, but Father
shoved her away with the barrel, aimed
while Livy choked out, *"Khk! Khk!"* He
squeezed the trigger. Winnie, directly
under, went deaf in the explosion,
blind as she saw her sister's head burst
like a spray of calla lilies tossed suddenly up
in the dark air. It took a moment for Winnie's
sight and hearing to return. She stared
open-mouthed at the thing in the dirt. After
a while Father said, "She'll stay down
this time, and no mistake. I'll get a spade."

44.

Boone woke and discovered that his dream
was no dream. Biddie was not there. And yet
he was unsurprised by this. It was as if she'd
visited him, his mind, in the night, told him
wordlessly how she loved him, how it was time
for her to die again now. Holding in his emotion,
he dressed in the dark, got one of the horses,
rode into town under an oddly-hued sky filled
with strange stars. When he arrived at the church
he knocked furiously until Father Synge
opened the door. "I need to see my wife,"
he said, marching past the Reverend. "But
Mr. Boone, as I told you..." He made his way
to the back, where he knew the coffin
was, and she was there, within it, beautiful
in death. He adjusted her hair slightly
while behind him Synge stared in amazement.
Boone gazed upon his wife's face for a long
time, the last time. "Thank you, Biddie," he
whispered to her at last, his tears touching
her cheeks. "Thank you for coming back
to me." He left the church then, alone.

45.

Everyone watched as the skies
seemed to calm, the mysterious colors
to fade, leaving behind an honest
Christian darkness and clear bright stars.
As it was quite cold, people began
to disperse, mumbling and muttering.
"A most peculiar thing." "What do
you suppose caused it?" In his room
Cyrus Drain resolved to pull on his coat,
go down to the tavern to cadge more
liquor and expound on his theory that
with the new century would come
the end of the world. Sheriff Ryder
said goodnight to the various townspeople,
happy there had been nothing for him
to do. Soon he and Miss String were left
alone in the silent street. "Everything's all right,
then?" she asked. He smiled. "It all seems
all right, Leonora," he said, "when you are
with me." Taking her arm, he led her to the door
of Mrs. Fenster's boardinghouse and said
goodnight. She smiled, and kissed him.

46.

Bewildered, Father Synge stared down at the face
of poor Mrs. Boone, returned now as mysteriously
as she'd gone, yet in different clothes, country clothes. He
shut the coffin lid, secured it. He would tell the sheriff,
he thought, walking back to his study. The strange night,
the bizarre colors, seemed to be waning—the sky
looked closer to normal now, the darkness becoming
black, the stars beginning to glow cold white again.
He saw motion in the churchyard and stepped
outside to see. It was Morris Levitt. The Reverend
moved quickly to the unfortunate man, saw
that his fingers were clotted with dirt, that he'd
scratched his way a few inches into the soil
of his mother's grave. "She's trying to get
out!" the journalist cried. Synge crouched,
held the weeping man gently in his arms. He listened.
After a while he was able to say, "No, lad. Not
anymore. Put your ear to the ground." Levitt
did. "She's still again," Father Synge assured him.
And, looking up, around the churchyard and to
where Mrs. Boone lay inside, he said: "I believe
they all are, now." The wind was cool on his face.

47.

Winnie lay breathless in her bed, terrified,
yet she knew she was perfectly safe. Father
had never in his life hit her, abused her, berated
her. That had all been for her sister. And now Livy
was gone, gone forever, buried under the earth
as she had been before. Winnie did not cry because
she felt that if she started, she would never stop—
never in this world. "He needn't have done it,"
she whispered into the night, to no one. "He needn't."
She realized what he hadn't, that Livy had been
dying again, that if the black rain had somehow
brought her back, the strange lights returned
her once more to her grave. She didn't know
why. She guessed no one would ever know
why It was over, anyway. She could hear Father
snoring in his bedroom. "I'm sorry, Livy," she
said. "I'm so sorry." Her body began to tremble.
Her heart pounded. This was her life, she thought.
This house. This farm. This man. She would
never know another. She closed her eyes,
tried to imagine Livy next to her, breathing or
not breathing. The bed was cold. She was cold.

48.

The next morning was quiet and clear
in Hardgrove, Nebraska. Red-winged blackbirds
fluttered on telegraph lines. Brown hawks
circled the blue sky. Mr. Sandstone's Emporium
opened on time, and the Farm & Feed,
the blacksmith's, the library. Sheriff Ryder
received a report from a woman who came
into his office of a dead body out near
the train tracks. He and a couple of men took
a wagon, picked up the corpse. Ryder recognized
his prisoner, who had no identification and so
would be buried in a pauper's grave. Cyrus Drain
watched them bring the stranger back, drank
from his bottle, said nothing. Morris Levitt
wrote up the story, and the story about the previous
night's "unprecedented astronomical occurrences,"
leaving out anything about an unquiet cemetery
or a newspaperman digging in the dirt. On the outskirts
of town, Winnie gathered eggs while her father rode off
to the tavern. Boone drank his morning coffee a bit
later than usual, then stood and went outside to work,
hammering nails into the slats of a loose barn door.

49.

Mrs. Boone was buried in a simple ceremony.
A young woman named Anna waited in
a hotel lobby some two hundred miles away for
a man she'd never known, who never came.
In the early summer Miss String became
Mrs. Ryder, and the newlyweds bought a lovely
blue house just off the main street. One day
Lucas Wheeler's daughter Winifred came to see
the sheriff and told him in a shaking voice
that her father had lied, her sister Livy had not gone
to stay with relatives in the city as he'd said. When
it was over the Ryders, unable to have children
of their own, adopted the girl, put her in school
again, loved her. Gideon Boone farmed on alone
for a few years, then quietly passed. Father Synge
discovered him on a visit, saw to it he was buried
with dignity next to his wife. Morris Levitt
wrote articles and finally left the county for parts
unknown. Cyrus Drain lived to be ninety,
enjoyed perfect health until the day he died.
No one else ever saw any strange phenomena
in the skies over Hardgrove, Nebraska.

50.

Nobody today remembers the night of black rain
in Hardgrove, when they came back.
Nobody remembers Hardgrove either, which
no longer exists, or even Jackson County, which
now is listed as one of the state's ghost counties,
referred to on a few old state documents but with
no specific records about it, not even quite
where it was. Hardgrove and Jackson blew away
in the Nebraska wind, covered over by so much
twentieth century dust. No copy of the
Jackson County Chronicle survived, so
the night of black rain is obliterated from history,
like the names of Gideon and Obedience Boone,
Morris Levitt, Father Synge. In the '30s a Winifred
Ryder formed a teacher's college in North Platte
which exists to this day, but nobody knows if she
was Winnie Wheeler from Hardgrove. Nebraska's
rain and stars have remained quite normal for over
a hundred years now. True, occasionally a tourist
does report an odd black glow emanating from the soil
just off one spot by the Interstate, late at night.
Driver fatigue, no doubt. Rest, then drive on.

ABOUT THE AUTHOR

Christopher Conlon is best known as the editor of the Bram Stoker Award-winning Richard Matheson tribute anthology *He Is Legend*. His first two novels, *Midnight on Mourn Street* and *A Matrix of Angels*, were both finalists for the Stoker Award, and he has written several collections of short stories and poems as well as a stage play. A former Peace Corps Volunteer, Conlon holds an M.A. in American Literature from the University of Maryland. He lives in the Washington, D.C. area. Visit his website at http://www.christopherconlon.com.

ABOUT THE PHOTOGRAPHER

Roberta Lannes-Sealey's photography has appeared in *JPG Magazine* and her artwork in *Cemetery Dance*. She has designed CD covers and app splash screens, as well as doing website graphics and design. As a writer she's published many stories of science fiction, fantasy, and horror, including her collection *The Mirror of Night* (under the name Roberta Lannes). She lives in the Santa Clarita Valley outside Los Angeles with her husband Mark Keynton Sealey, a British poet, journalist, and music critic. Her images can be purchased through her online gallery at http://www.lannes-sealey.com.

www.ingramcontent.com/pod-product-compliance
Lightning Source LLC
Chambersburg PA
CBHW060132260626
47160CB00005B/2078